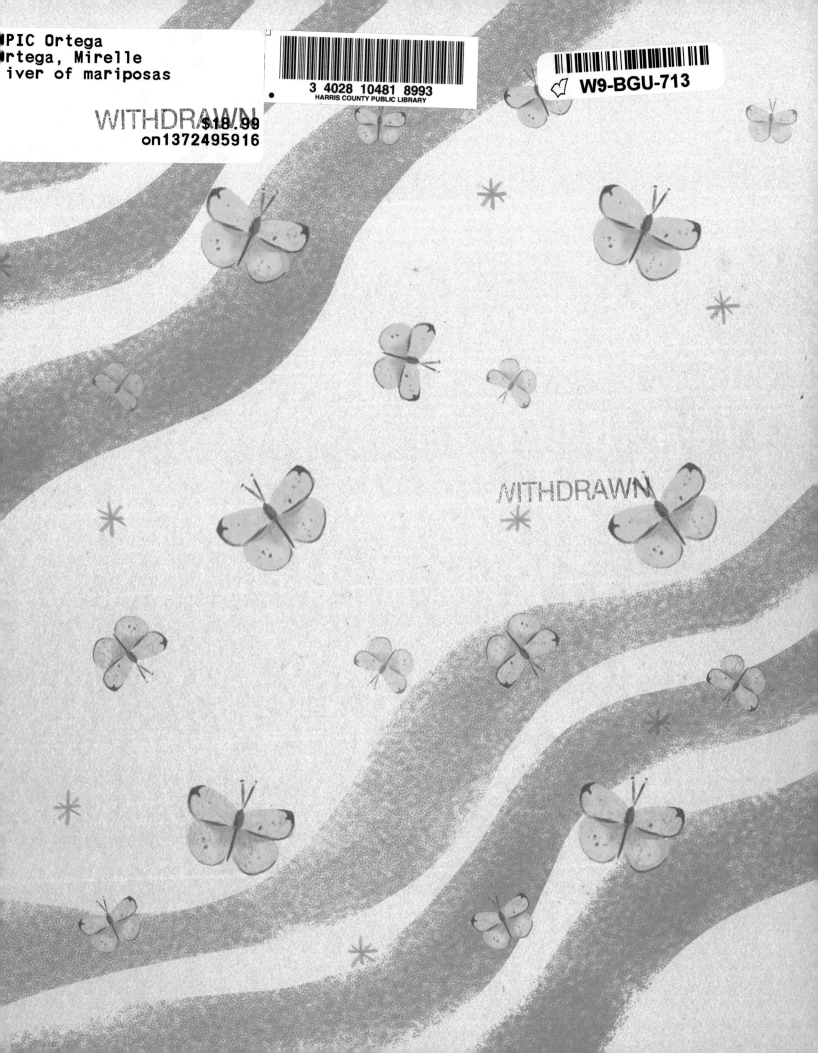

PIC Ortega
Ortega, Mirelle
iver of mariposas

WITHDRAWN
$18.99
on1372495916

3 4028 10481 8993
HARRIS COUNTY PUBLIC LIBRARY

W9-BGU-713

WITHDRAWN

Al río de las mariposas y a quienes lo cuidan.
—M.O.

Copyright © 2023 Mirelle Ortega

Book design by Melissa Nelson Greenberg

Published in 2023 by CAMERON + COMPANY, a division of ABRAMS.
All rights reserved. No portion of this book may be reproduced, stored in a retrieval system,
or transmitted in any form or by any means, mechanical, electronic, photocopying,
recording, or otherwise, without written permission from the publisher.

Library of Congress Cataloging-in-Publication Data available.
ISBN: 978-1-4197-6061-7

Printed in China

10 9 8 7 6 5 4 3 2 1

CAMERON KIDS is an imprint of CAMERON + COMPANY

**CAMERON + COMPANY**
Petaluma, California
www.cameronbooks.com

# RIVER of MARIPOSAS

## MIRELLE ORTEGA

cameron kids

Can you imagine a time when the land and the sky belonged to the mariposas? I can. Way back, before the people came, there were so many, the river itself was named after them.

I used to watch the butterflies fly around the ixoras in my godmother's garden, and, carried by the gentle wind, float above the Papaloapan River. The river of butterflies.

I dreamed about that time before the cities were built, and the butterflies found new lands and new paths to get to them.

I shared my dream, but no one could picture a sky full of butterflies like I did. So, I decided to show them.

This year, on my birthday, I would bring back the mariposas. Mamá, Papá, and I got to work. For days and nights we drew, painted, cut, and glued paper butterflies. Big and small, bright and shiny, we worked and worked until we had so many we could no longer fit them in the living room.

And when the big day came, I was so happy.
My favorite song, "Cielito Lindo," played from
the kitchen as Mamá made tres leches cake and
pambazos for our guests.

Papá and I danced our way outside, carrying
big boxes of paper butterflies.

We placed them all around the trees, hanging high
and low, dancing in the wind, until the dream inside
my head came to life.

Truly satisfied, we looked at our hard work,
the garden alive with paper butterflies.

But then, a cold wind made the wind chimes sing, and we looked up to the sky, just in time for us to see the first dark cloud.

And as quick as the wind, the clear blue sky turned to gray. A thick summer rain cloud hung heavy above our heads.

Then, the first raindrop hit the ground.

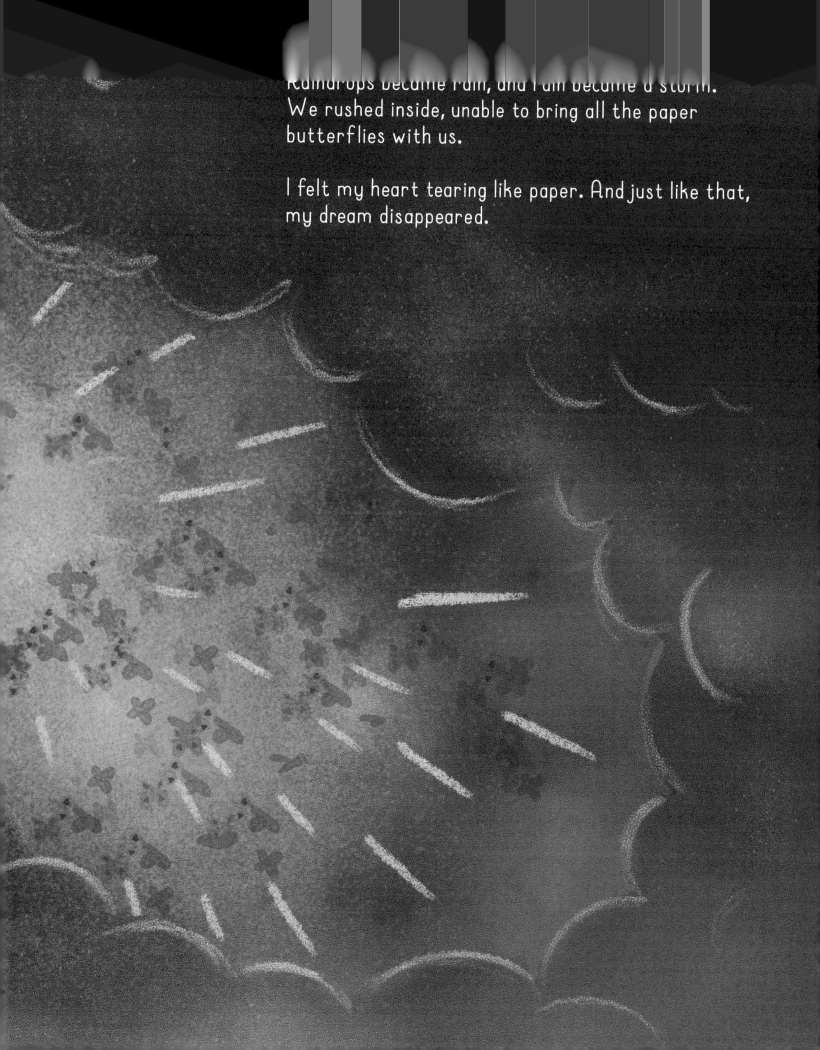

Raindrops became rain, and rain became a storm. We rushed inside, unable to bring all the paper butterflies with us.

I felt my heart tearing like paper. And just like that, my dream disappeared.

I hid in my room and closed my eyes to form a
cocoon. After the storm, Mamá and Papá came
knocking on my door, the same way sunrays knock on
a chrysalis, asking for the butterfly to come.

But I was busy brewing
a storm of my own.

"Hija, don't be sad," said Mamá, "think of the butterflies. Do you think they let a little rain ruin their plans?"

I knew Mamá was onto something. So, I emerged to warm hugs from Mamá and Papá. "The storm can take the paper butterflies," said Papá, "but don't let it take your dream. Canta y no llores."

CIENTOS DE MARIPOSAS AMARILLAS

Papá turned on the radio to cheer me up, but I couldn't help but feel sad all over again, thinking of the beauty I wasn't able to share.

And then, as I reached to pick up a pair of paper wings, it flew away! It was a real butterfly. And then another one, and another one!

The storm had brought my dream to life—
the mariposas were back.

…UZAN LA CIUDAD DESVIADAS POR LA TORMENTA

Their delicate wings fluttered, and my eyes followed them up into the clear blue sky. The sky was filled with thousands of yellow butterflies.

A river of mariposas amarillas, flowing with the wind, as far as I could see.

One by one, neighbors filled the street, looking up in awe. Then we danced, we laughed, and we even thanked the rain.

It was just like the before times, when the land and the sky belonged to the butterflies.

Do you remember that summer? When the mariposas came back? I do.

# Author's Note

I was very small when a teacher first taught me about the Papaloapan River. Cutting through the state of Veracruz and flowing into the Gulf of Mexico, the river—named by natives Papaloapan, a Nahuatl word that translates to "the river of butterflies"—breathes life into the land. The meaning of the name stuck with me; I imagined a floating river of butterflies.

At the time that felt like an impossible dream, but as it turns out, sometimes things that seem impossible are just unlikely. Unlikely things, dear reader, sometimes do happen. Many years after first hearing the words "river of butterflies" in a classroom, I stepped out of a plane in Veracruz on a hot summer day and found myself surrounded by hundreds of yellow butterflies, caught in a real-life river of mariposas. That August in 2017, people all across towns and cities in the state of Veracruz found themselves similarly awestruck by the arrival of thousands of butterflies after Hurricane Franklin disrupted their usual migration path. The event captured the imaginations of many across the state, including mine. Riding in my dad's truck as he drove us back home, my eyes were glued to the yellow river flowing across the bright orange afternoon sky— a dream come true.

 MIRELLE

MARIPOSA AMARILLA

IXORAS

West Indian Jasmine

PAMBAZO

A Mexican snack made with pambazo bread – yum!

TRES LECHES CAKE

A sponge cake soaked in three kinds of milk – ¡Delicioso!

"CIELITO LINDO"

A popular traditional Mexican song by Quirino Mendoza y Cortés, which means "pretty sweetheart."

Harris County Public Library
Houston, Texas

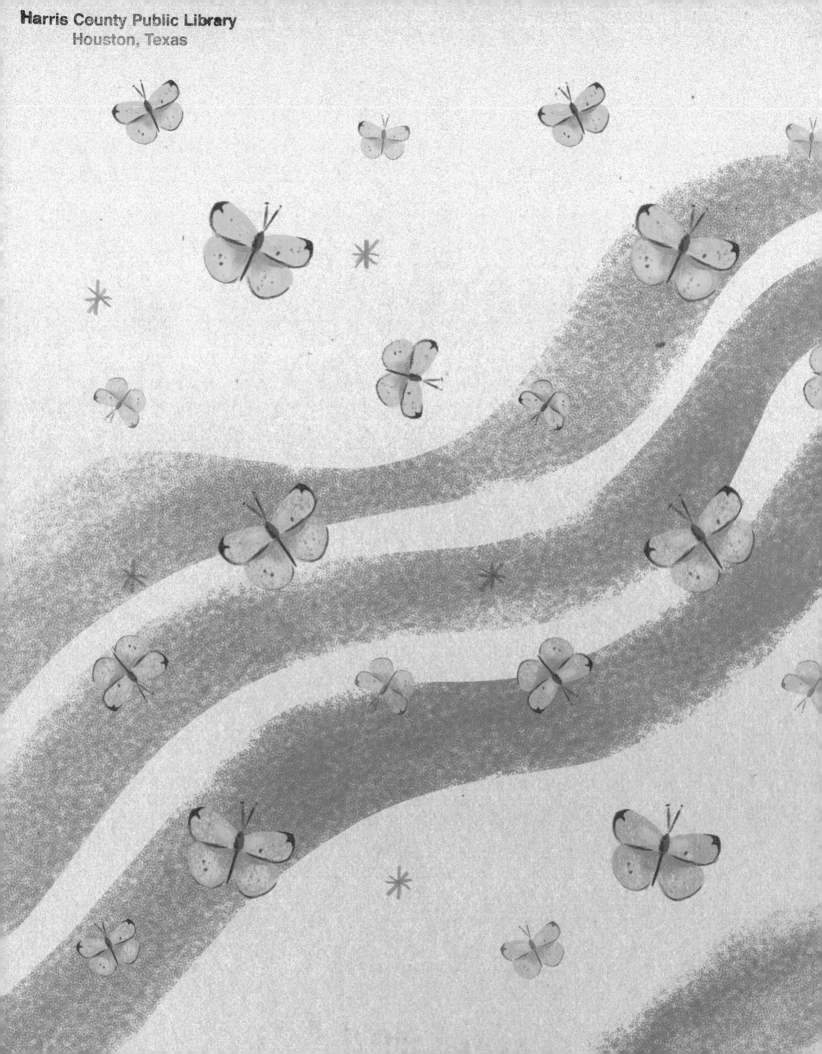